The Witches House
By Anthony Uyl

Devoted Publishing
Woodstock, Ontario, 2017

The Witches House

By Anthony Uyl

What kind of stories do you have?
Let us know!

Visit our website: www.devotedpublishing.com
Contact us at: devotedpub@hotmail.com
Visit us on Facebook: @DevotedPublishing

Published in Woodstock, Ontario, Canada 2017

For bulk theatrical rates, please contact us at the above email address.

ISBN: 978-1-77356-093-9

Act 1

INT. - DARK ROOM - DAY

The room is lit with candles and in the middle of the room is a table with an altar on top of it. An upside down cross is hung above the altar and blood soaks the cross and is dripping down onto the altar.

In front of the altar is MOM in a black priestly robe with gold decoration. She is on her knees praying.

MOM:
I have sent them to you my lady.

Silence.

MOM:
They should arrive at your house at any moment.

Silence.

MOM:
Do you have any other wishes my lady?

BLOODY MARY (V.O.):
(in a scratchy voice)
You have done well my servant.

MOM:
I wish nothing more than to please you.

BLOODY MARY (V.O.):
Which you have done.

MOM:
What else would you have me do?

BLOODY MARY (V.O.):
Go to your home and wait for the appointed time. When that comes you will come back to me and offer me the final sacrifice.

MOM:
Yes, my lady. What ever you wish will be my command.

BLOODY MARY (V.O.):
Very well then, go and wait.

MOM:
Yes, my lady.

Mom remains kneeling.

EXT. - CAR - DAY

The Witches House
    The car is stuck in bumper to bumper traffic on an interstate. The distortions in the air from the heat can be seen coming from the traffic.

INT. - CAR – DAY

    Four young people are in the car. Two girls and two guys.

    DAVID and AMY, who are dating, are sitting in the front. Amy, who is driving, is visibly frustrated and David is looking down at a map.

    GREG and CARLY, who are also dating are sitting in the back. Greg and Carly are sitting quietly just waiting for the trip to be over.

    AMY:
    (slams the steering wheels with the palms of her hands)
Damn it! Where is the cut-off?

    DAVID:
    (holds up his hand as though he's trying to reassure Amy)
It should be coming up anytime now.

    AMY:
You've been saying that for an hour now.

    DAVID:
    (frustrated)
Hey calm down, it's not my fault we got stuck in rush hour traffic.

    AMY:
Well you're not helping the situation any.

    DAVID:
Do you need some coffee? You usually get cranky when you haven't had your caffeine fix.

    A car honks its' horn.

    AMY:
    (yells into the rear-view mirror)
Shut up. Get a life asshole.

    GREG:
Dude your girl is starting to scare me.

    DAVID:
She gets like this when she gets mad.

    GREG:
Seeing as I've never seen her angry this is kinda freaky.

    DAVID:
You haven't seen anything, just wait till she's PMSing.

    CARLY:
(in a high pitched, annoyed voice)
Hey that was uncalled for.

    AMY:
    (to Carly)
Thanks hun, at least someone supports me in this car.

DAVID:
(raises his hand in a defensive gesture)
Hey I never said I didn't. But you getting crank is something else.

AMY:
(slams the steering wheel with her right hand)
You've been with me for two years and just now you're telling me this?

DAVID:
(looking down at map)
Didn't think it was important.

AMY:
(glaring at David)
Anything else you're hiding from me?

DAVID:
Not that I'm going to admit to now.

AMY:
What's that supposed to mean?

GREG:
(looking out his window)
Well isn't this great, a domestic in the middle of rush hour traffic.

CARLY:
Shhh.

DAVID:
(to Amy)
It's not supposed to mean anything, I was just trying to lighten the mood.

AMY:
(looking forward)
Well you're not doing too well at it.

DAVID:
(looks back at map and puts his hands on the map trying to locate where they are)
Can we just drop this and get back to the trip? So what's with this house
we're supposed to be going to?

AMY:
(sighs)
Fine, it's an old Victorian mansion.

CARLY:
(to Amy)
So how did we end up staying here?

AMY:
My mom offered it to us. Apparently a friend of hers owns the plantation and she said it was okay that
we stay here for our trip.

GREG:
(looking out window)
Sounds kind of boring.

AMY:
(looking forward)
Well I don't plan on staying on the plantation much.

The Witches House
>DAVID:

How far away is the city?

>AMY:

Not far, we could take a cab there fairly easily.

>DAVID:
>*(looks at Amy with eyebrows raised)*

Why would we take a cab when we have a car?

>AMY:

Well HUN...
>*(with emphasis)*

... I'm not really in the mood to be drinking and driving. Do you really want to spend a weekend with me if I get charged?

>DAVID:
>*(excited)*

Cab it is.

>AMY:

Good boy.

>*A GHOST that looks like a rotting, decaying man wearing a Victorian suit is seen sitting between Carly and Greg.*

>DAVID (V.O.):

So we're past this?

>*The ghost looks at Greg and then Carly.*

>AMY (V.O.):

No, you'll get what's coming to you later when there aren't witnesses around.

>*Ghost Vanishes.*

>GREG:

That doesn't sound good.

>DAVID:

That is never a good thing.

>AMY:

It's good to see that you've figured that out.

>DAVID:

I was forewarned.

>GREG:
>*(cringes)*

Uh oh.

>AMY:

By who?

>DAVID:
>*(scared)*

Uh people.

>*Amy hits the brakes causing everyone to lurch forward.*

AMY:
(angrily)
What people?

DAVID:
(defensively)
Well your mom for one, and your ex.
AMY:
(screaming)
My mom Why would you let her say that?

DAVID:
I didn't take her seriously at the time, maybe I should have.

AMY:
Excuse me?

DAVID:
(points out the window)
Hey let's not do this now, look there's the exit we need right there.

Cars are honking their horns. Amy looks and starts to drive towards the ramp.

AMY:
(calmly)
What else did my mom tell you?

DAVID:
Nothing.

AMY:
(eyes narrow looking at David)
Why don't I believe you?

DAVID:
You know as well as I do that your mom is crazy as a loon. I didn't think she was serious about it. She honestly didn't say anything else. Okay?

AMY:
Fine, but I still don't believe you.

EXT. - CAR - DAY

The car pulls off the interstate and starts heading down an open country road. There are a few farms along the road but not many. The area is mainly empty fields with nothing growing in them. They are mainly overgrown with weeds that give the fields a sinister look.

The car pulls into a small village that looks run down. They drive down the main street and see many of the buildings have been closed and boarded up.

Some dirt blows in a small whirlwind across the road and the car pulls through it all.

INT. - CAR – DAY

GREG:
(looking out the window)
This is kinda creepy.

DAVID:
Yeah no kidding.

The Witches House
   Amy turns the steering wheel into a small general store. The parking lot is full of grass growing through cracks in the pavement and is filled with dirt. The parking spaces are barely visible but Amy manages to pull the car into a spot with moderate success.

   Amy starts to get out of car.

   DAVID:
   (surprised)
Where are you going?

   AMY:
I'm going to ask for directions.

   DAVID:
   (hesitantly)
We got a map, I'm sure we can find it.

   AMY:
   (looking at David with eyebrows raised)
Your navigation skills leave something to be desired. Besides it'll only take a second.

   DAVID:
   (rolls his eyes)
Fine....
   (pause)
... My navigation skills are fine by the way.

   GREG:
Sorry dude, but I have to agree with Amy here.

   DAVID:
   (to Greg)
Hey. Traitor.

   Amy gets out of the car and heads into the small general store.

INT. - GENERAL STORE - DAY

   The general store is dirty and grimy, a reflection of what the town looks like outside.

   There is a store clerk behind the counter with a five o'clock shadow. There isn't much on the shelves.

   Amy walks up to the counter where the STORE CLERK is.

   STORE CLERK:
   (enthusiastically)
Can I help you?

   AMY:
Yeah, hi, I was wondering if you could help me with some directions.

   STORE CLERK:
   (with a smile)
Sure.

   AMY:
I'm looking for the old McMann plantation on Grimsby Line.

   STORE CLERK:
   (shocked)
Oh.

AMY:
What?

STORE CLERK:
(reassuringly)
Oh nothing.

AMY:
(hesitantly)
Yeah, okay...
(pause)
...anyway, what's the easiest way to get there?

STORE CLERK:
(calmly)
It wouldn't hurt you to stay away from there.

AMY:
(angrily)
Excuse me?

STORE CLERK:
I've been here a long time and everyone that was here agrees that t he McMann plantation is a place you just don't go. Even the daring teenagers in the nearby city don't dare to go there.

AMY:
Why is that?

STORE CLERK:
Strange things have happened there.

AMY:
What kind of things?

STORE CLERK:
I can't really say.

AMY:
It sounds like a bunch of old wives tales to me.

STORE CLERK:
Please I'm warning you, stay away from there.

AMY:
I'll make up my mind when we get there. Now are you going to help me or not?

STORE CLERK:
(sighs)
Fine, head down this road for two miles. Grimsby Line intersects the road there. You want to head left and head to the end of the road. The McMann plantation is the last place on the road. You can't miss it.

AMY:
How much longer till we get there?

STORE CLERK:
About another twenty minutes.

AMY:
Sounds simple enough.

The Witches House

STORE CLERK:
Please I'm begging you one last time, stay away from there. Get back in your car with your friends and just go to the city and stay there.

AMY:
Hey, we're students who don't have a lot of money. We've been offered free housing here and we're going to take it. Unless you're going to open up your home to us?

STORE CLERK:
You don't want to stay there.

AMY:
Then leave it alone, we'll be fine, we can take care of ourselves.

STORE CLERK:
Alright, if that's what you want. But God help you.

AMY:
Thanks, but I'm an atheist.

Amy leaves and heads back to the car.

STORE CLERK:
You may not be for much longer.

As the door closes a shadow falls on the store clerk revealing him to be decayed and rotting. As the shadow passes he is gone.

EXT. - HOUSE – DAY

The car with Amy, David, Greg and Carly in it is traveling down a dirt road. The fields around them are barren and brown. A dust cloud follows the car as they travel down the road. Gusts of wind add to the dirt being thrown up in the air. Vultures are also see circling the car as it travels down the road.

As the car pulls up they see a lavish house surrounded by green grass and trees. As they get closer to the foliage it can been seen that the trees are covered in vines and the grass is mostly weeds.

INT. - HOUSE - DAY

Looking out a window view from the house into the drive way, the WITCH stands watching the car. She is dressed in brown tattered robes and has a slight hump when she stands. Her hands are holding the curtains and they are weathered and frail.

The car stops, Amy, David, Greg and Carly all get out and the witch moves away.

EXT. - HOUSE - DAY

Amy, David, Carly and Greg pull up to the house where it can be seen. It is very well maintained and looks very welcoming.

GREG:
Is this it?

AMY:
It would appear to be.

CARLY:
This is a nice place. Looks like we hit the jackpot.

AMY:
Not according to that guy back in the village.

DAVID:
I wouldn't worry about that. He's probably just trying to get under our skin.

AMY:
It didn't seem like it, it was like he was genuinely trying to warn me about something.

DAVID:
Oh come on. We've come all this way and you want to turn back now? Look at this place. It's beautiful. Who wouldn't want to stay here?

David holds out his hand towards Amy. Amy takes his hand and smiles.

AMY:
Yeah you're right. Let's go see what's inside.

David and Amy begin walking up to the house arm in arm.

GREG:
Look at those two, now walking arm in arm. They sure made up fast.

CARLY:
They didn't make up at all. They just skipped the whole kiss and make up stage and went back to everything being normal.

GREG:
Those two baffle me.

CARLY:
I think it's romantic. Whatever those two say to each other they still show they love each other no matter what.

GREG:
You trying to hint at something?

CARLY:
Not at all.

GREG:
I'll say it when I'm ready.

CARLY:
And when will that be? I've been waiting for a long time now.

GREG:
It's only been a couple of months.

CARLY:
Yeah, a couple of months since I said it. Remember the awkwardness after that? Remember you saying that you would tell me you loved me when you were ready?

GREG:
Yeah, I remember.

CARLY:
When will that day come?

GREG:
Soon, maybe, I don't know.

CARLY:
Well that's so reassuring.

The Witches House

GREG:
Isn't it enough to know that I really really like you? And that I'll do everything I can to make you happy?

CARLY:
Sometimes a girl needs more than that.

GREG:
I'm just scared.

CARLY:
Of what?

GREG:
I'm not sure.

CARLY:
Well figure it out soon. I'm not going to wait around forever.

Carly walks off towards Amy and David.

GREG:
Women.

Greg joins Carly, Amy and David.

AMY:
So shall we go take a look?

DAVID:
Sure, I'll go grab our bags. Greg you wanna grab yours and Carly's?

GREG:
You make it sound like I'm her bitch.

CARLY:
You mean you're not?

GREG:
Ha ha, very funny.

DAVID:
C'mon bitch let's get the girls things.

Greg groans then follows David to the car.

AMY:
So did you talk with Greg?

CARLY:
Yeah, kind of.

AMY:
And?

CARLY:
What do you think?

AMY:
Oh babe, I'm so sorry.

CARLY:
I can keep hoping can't I?

AMY:
Yeah I guess, but for how long?

CARLY:
Yeah, my patience is starting to wear thin.

David and Greg rejoin the girls with suitcases in their arms.

DAVID:
Are we ready to go in?

AMY:
Sure are.

GREG:
What were you girls talking about?

Carly smiles and looks at Greg flirtatiously.

CARLY:
Nothing you need to worry about.

Amy, David, Greg and Carly walk up to the front door. A faint wind can be heard blowing through the nearby trees and the shutters on the windows.

DAVID:
Where did she say the key was?

AMY:
She said it was under the windowsill.

Amy begins feeling under the right side windowsill.

AMY:
Here it is.

Amy pulls out a small black box and heads to the front door.

GREG:
Great, let's get inside.

Amy unlocks the door.

INT. - HOUSE – DAY

The group walks in to the house into a large foyer. The ceiling reaches into the second story and a balcony surrounds the room. There are a few doors on the ground level leading to other rooms. There is a large double set of doors at the far end of the room.

A dual set of stairs go up to the balcony on each side of the foyer. There are also two hallways the lead off from the right and left of the foyer. In front of the stairs are tables that have some books and empty vases.

The sound of the gust of wind blows through the foyer. There are paintings on the walls of people the group doesn't know. Along the left hand wall is a large mirror which Carly goes and checks herself in.

GREG:
Wow look at this place. How did your mom get to know people that had this dig?

The Witches House
> AMY:
> *(surprised)*
I have no idea...
> *(pause)*
...I'm as shocked as you are.

> DAVID:
Where do you figure the rooms are?

> AMY:
Umm, my mom said they were upstairs along the balcony. I guess we just pick one.

> *Amy looks over at one of the paintings and stares at it intently.*

> DAVID:
What's wrong?

> AMY:
That painting, he looks familiar.

> DAVID:
Like who?

> AMY:
Believe it or not, looks like the guy I got directions from.

> DAVID:
Maybe he's a relative.

> AMY:
Yeah, maybe.

> *The group heads upstairs and open the door to one of the bedrooms.*

INT. - BEDROOM - DAY

> *In the bedroom is a lavishly decorated room with drapes, wardrobes and a king size bed.*

> Greg (V.O):
Is there any food here? I'm kinda hungry.

> AMY:
There should be, the kitchen is just through the double doors in the foyer.

> GREG:
Awesome.

> *The group puts their bags in their rooms and then they head down to the kitchen.*

INT. - KITCHEN – DAY

> *The kitchen is fully updated with stainless steel appliances and solid oak cupboards. There is no mess, the kitchen is spotlessly clean. Amy opens the pantry and sees that it is full of food.*

> AMY:
Well the pantry is full, guess we have nothing to worry about here.

> CARLY:
Look at this kitchen...
> *(pause)*
... I'm in total awe, I gotta find out who owns this place and hook up with him.

GREG:
(annoyed)
Hey. I'm standing right here.

CARLY:
Your point?

Greg grumbles before reaching up and grabbing a bag of chips and begins to eat. Amy walks up to one of the cupboards and opens it up. When she opens it a splattered blood stain is on the inside of the cupboard door. She fails to notice it and just smiles as she sees more food stacked in the cupboard.

AMY:
Well it was nice of the owners to make sure there was food here before they left, makes it easier for us.

DAVID:
Yeah for sure.
(pause)
So what do we want to do?

AMY:
Well, I don't know about you...but I'm getting dressed and heading out to a club. You losers can stay here if you want.

CARLY:
I'm up for that.

DAVID:
I think we all are.

INT. - NIGHT CLUB - NIGHT

They arrive at a night club where there is loud techno music playing. The dance floor is crowded with people dancing around. There are booths on raised platforms that are on either side of the dance floor that have people sitting in them. Some of these people are making out with each other while others seem to be playing drinking games. Lasers shoot through the air giving in to more of the techno feeling of the club.

The group walks in and manages to find an empty booth in which Amy and Carly sit down in. David and Greg head off to the bar to get drinks.

DAVID:
What's your problem?

GREG:
Oh, nothing.

DAVID:
Yeah, you're not a good liar man.

GREG:
Carly is asking me about the whole love thing again.

DAVID:
Is it really that hard to say you love her?

GREG:
(angrily)
Yeah, okay? It is.

DAVID:
Alright, but it's pretty obvious how you feel.

The Witches House

GREG:
I'm just not ready.

DAVID:
Alright.

David and Greg get their drinks from the bartender then head back to the booth where Amy and Carly are waiting. Amy takes a quick drink from her drink and then stands up and holds out her hand to David.

AMY:
Let's dance.

DAVID:
Sure, I'm not used to girls being so forward.

AMY:
(smiles)
Get used to it buddy.

David takes a drink from his beer and heads out to the dance floor being pulled by Amy. Greg sits down and Carly snuggles up beside him. She looks him in the eyes then sighs.

AMY:
You think those two will ever work on how they feel with each other?

DAVID:
It's pretty obvious how they feel but for some reason they can't just come forward with it.

AMY:
It's more him than her.

DAVID:
She's said it?

AMY:
Yeah.

DAVID:
No wonder things are awkward between them.

AMY:
Shush, enough of them, right now it's just about you and me.

The two of them start dancing with each other. They are grinding with each other and also kissing passionately.

While they are kissing a rotted hand is seen reaching in behind Amy's head. Just as they finish kissing Amy leans her head back nearly touching the hand. David sees something and suddenly pulls Amy away. She seems surprised at this sudden action and lets out a scream.

The hand disappears as soon as David pulls her away.

AMY:
What was that all about?

DAVID:
Nothing, I thought I saw someone behind you.

AMY:
Thanks I guess.

They kiss again.

INT. - HOUSE – BEDROOM - NIGHT

Amy and David are getting naked and jumping in the bed. They kiss and rub up against each other.

They groan in pleasure as they begin to have sex.

At first they do it doggy-style and then she mounts him and begins to ride him.

They don't notice the witch standing in the window silhouetted against the moon-lit sky.

They keep having sex until Amy turns her head and suddenly grasps and pulls the covers over her naked body.

DAVID:
What?

AMY:
I thought I saw someone.

DAVID:
Where?

AMY:
It was nothing, I was just hallucinating.

DAVID:
That good huh?

AMY:
You have no idea.

INT. - KITCHEN - NIGHT

The sex finishes and Amy gets up and leaves the room with a robe on. She walks to the kitchen, opens up the fridge and pulls out a bottle of water and begins to drink it.

A noise like a crowd of people is heard beyond the kitchen. Amy looks surprised and goes out to investigate.

INT. - DINING ROOM – NIGHT

When she enters the room she sees a room full of people wearing Victorian suits and lavish gowns. There are men and women of all ages. Some are dancing others are sitting at a table and others are standing on stairs on both sides of the room. There is no food or music playing.

Upon a closer look she sees that the people are decayed and rotting. Some are missing eyes while others are missing entire limbs. She watches in horror for a few minutes before dropping her bottle of water and running out of the room. One of the ghosts looks in the direction she was revealing himself to be the store clerk Amy had got directions from. He smiles and returns to the ghostly party.

INT. - BEDROOM – NIGHT

Amy bursts in to her and David's bedroom.

AMY:
    (yelling)
We have to get out of here.

The Witches House
DAVID:
Whoa, what's wrong?

AMY:
This house, it's...there are things here.

DAVID:
What are you talking about?

AMY:
In the room beyond the kitchen. Go and see for yourself.

DAVID:
Alright, let's go check it out.

INT. - FOYER – NIGHT

As Amy and David exit the room, Greg and Carly come flying out their room screaming.

DAVID:
Hey, what's wrong?

CARLY:
We saw something in our room.

DAVID:
Like what?

GREG:
It was a walking decayed corpse in a suit.

DAVID:
(in disbelief)
You too?

CARLY:
It's true.

David takes a look in their room and sees nothing.

DAVID:
There's nothing there now.

Greg and Carly look in their room and see nothing in there.

CARLY:
Well there was something in there.

DAVID:
Sure.

GREG:
Believe us or not, we're out of here.

DAVID:
Just hang on a second I'm going to check something out.

GREG:
Well, we're going with you.

DAVID:
If you want.

INT. - DINING ROOM - NIGHT

David, Greg and Carly all go to the kitchen and into the dining room.

When they open the doors they see the bottle of water that Amy dropped and some empty tables but the ghosts are gone. Greg and Carly are apprehensive about coming into the room but take a look anyway.

DAVID:
See, nothing here.

GREG:
There is something here, I'm telling you.

DAVID:
I'm sorry, but I think you've just had too much to drink.

GREG:
Booze doesn't make you hallucinate.

DAVID:
Are you sure booze is all you took at the club?

GREG:
That's not funny dude, I'm not a doper and you know that.

INT. - FOYER – NIGHT

As they walk back into the foyer, Amy is waiting for them by the front door with her and David's suitcases. She is standing with her arms crossed, looking scared.

DAVID:
What's going on?

AMY:
We're leaving.

DAVID:
What? Why?

AMY:
That should be obvious.

DAVID:
There's nothing here.

AMY:
(crying)
Yes there is, and I'm not staying here another second.

DAVID:
Alright, if you want.

Amy turns around to the doors and grabs the door handle to open it. The handle won't move and the door won't open. Amy pulls harder and harder but it doesn't move.

DAVID:
Here let me try.

David tries to open the door but he too is unsuccessful.

They turn just as Greg is seen throwing one of the vases on the side table at the window.

The Witches House
>   AMY:
No wait.

>   *The vase shatters against the window but the window doesn't break. The vases shatters to mist and they watch as the vase reforms itself on the table Greg took it from.*

>   GREG:
Holy shit, see man there's something going on here.

>   DAVID:
Alright, let's stay calm and try to find a way out of here.

>   AMY:
I don't think we're going to be able to find a way out.

>   CARLY:
I don't like this.

>   DAVID:
Let's not try to be so negative, this has all got to be a sick joke.

>   *As they turn around in the foyer the witch in brown robes is seen at the top of the balcony.*

>   DAVID:
Hey wait. Who are you?

>   *The witch starts to move off.*

>   DAVID:
Where are you going? I want to talk to you.

>   *David chases the witch up the stairs but finds nothing when he gets to the stop of the stairs.*

>   DAVID:
Where'd she go?

Act 2

INT. - HALLWAY - NIGHT

The group is walking through the house. They walk down a dark hallway with the moon shining through a large window at the end of the hallway. Doors line the hall along both sides and their shadows darken the floor as they move.

AMY:
Can we turn some lights on please?

David goes to a light switch and tries to turn it on, nothing happens.

DAVID:
Looks like the power is out.

CARLY:
Great that makes this all the better.

AMY:
We should have taken some flashlights.

GREG:
I wouldn't be surprised if this house didn't have any.

CARLY:
Why do you have to be so negative?

GREG:
(sarcastically)
I'm so sorry.

AMY:
(angrily)
There's no need to get like that.

GREG:
Okay, I'm just scared.

CARLY:
We all are.

AMY:
Which is why there's no need to be going and aggravating each other.

GREG:
I wasn't trying to aggravate anybody.

DAVID:
Can we stop arguing please and focus on trying to find that person?

AMY:
Depends if we can all behave.

The Witches House
Greg rolls his eyes.

CARLY:
Who do you think that was?

DAVID:
I have no idea, but they probably know what's going on here.

A door creaks open.

DAVID:
Hello?....
(silence)
...is anybody there?

INT. - LIBRARY - NIGHT

David goes to look in the open door and finds an old library. The walls are filled with old books and in the center of the library sits an old desk that has a lamp and an old notebook. No one is in the room. There is a large window with a tree casting a silhouette over the dark room.

Lightning flashes causing everyone to jump. There is another door on a wall by the large window.

GREG:
You think someone's in there?

DAVID:
Doesn't look like it.

CARLY:
Doors just don't open on their own.

DAVID:
Could have been a gust of wind.

CARLY:
Maybe.

Greg goes into the room and looks around. He stands by the other door.

GREG:
There are no open windows.

DAVID:
Could have been anything then.

GREG:
Yeah, like a person.

DAVID:
But there's no one around.

GREG:
Why can't you accept that we're totally screwed?

AMY:
Oh for crying out loud.

GREG:
What?

AMY:
I want to get out of here as much as you do, but this attitude isn't helping

The door by the window suddenly bursts open and a ghost in a suit grabs Greg. The girls start to scream and Greg begins to yell and tries to fight off the ghost.

GREG:
(screaming)
Someone help me.

David runs up and tries to fight off the ghost but his hands pass right through it. Greg holds onto the bookcase on the wall and tries once more to fight off the ghost. After a few seconds the ghost finally gives up and Greg stumbles into the middle of the room.

GREG:
Where'd he go?

DAVID:
I don't know.

GREG:
He can't just have vanished.

DAVID:
Well apparently he did.

GREG:
This is just too messed up.

The lights start to flicker in the room. The group quickly gets out of the library and back into the hallway, the lights are flickering out there as well.

DAVID:
I never believed in haunted houses up until now.

AMY:
Neither did I.

GREG:
And you're the supreme atheist in the group.

AMY:
Yeah, I know.

DAVID:
We should keep moving.

CARLY:
To where? Where could we possibly go?

DAVID:
I don't know, but there has to be another way out of here.

CARLY:
Have you seen another way out?

DAVID:
No.

CARLY:
So what is the point of all this?

The Witches House

DAVID:
I don't know, but if we keep moving it's better than just sitting here.

AMY:
He's got a point hun.

CARLY:
But what if we encounter more of those things?

DAVID:
That's just a risk we're going to have to take.

Suddenly Greg is pulled back through the doorway in the library. It looks like he is being pulled back by something but they can't see what. A huge gust of wind accompanies the kidnapping causing everyone to duck for cover. The wind ends once Greg is gone.

GREG (V.O.):
Help me.

CARLY:
Greg.

Carly starts to run after Greg but is held back by Amy.

CARLY:
(crying)
We have to help him.

AMY:
We can't risk it.

CARLY:
We can't just leave him.

AMY:
We have to for now.

CARLY:
You don't understand.

AMY:
I'm sorry hun.

Carly begins to cry into Amy's shoulder. Eventually Carly collapses into Amy and they lead her off into the hallway. As they step out of the library a loud scream is heard.

CARLY:
(screaming)
Greg.

AMY:
So now what do we do?

DAVID:
I'm not sure, but I'm not leaving Greg.

AMY:
I know.

CARLY:
Damn right we're not leaving him.

AMY:
Where do you think he was taken to?

DAVID:
I'm not sure, but unless we want to be taken too, I suggest we keep moving.

The group heads down the hallway.

INT. - DINING ROOM - NIGHT

The group enters into the dining area where Amy saw all the ghosts. Carly is still crying and she walks up to one of the chairs and sits down. She begins to sob.

David and Amy hug. Amy begins to lightly cry and David tries to console her by rubbing her back.

After crying for a bit, Amy walks over to Carly and tries to comfort her.

CARLY:
(angrily)
No. Don't touch me.

AMY:
Hun, I was just trying to...

CARLY:
(angrily)
This is all your fault.

AMY:
(defensively)
How do you figure?

CARLY:
(angrily, she points a finger at Amy)
This was all your idea. This trip, it's your fault.

AMY:
You don't mean that.

CARLY:
Yes...I do. You wanted a weekend away to help your relationship, with, with...
(points and David)
...him. And now Greg has had to pay the price. I'm done with you, I'm going to find a way out of here myself.

Carly begins to walk off.

AMY:
(to David)
Do something.

DAVID:
What do you want me to do?

AMY:
I don't know.

INT. - KITCHEN – NIGHT

David runs after Carly and catches up to her in the kitchen.

The Witches House
>DAVID:
>*(to Carly)*

Okay, yes. It was our idea to come here. And we're sorry for that.
>*(Carly begins to cry again. Then glares at David)*

But we can't be off on our own in this place.

>CARLY:
>*(sadly)*

But I want to find him.

>DAVID:

I want to find him to. He was a good friend to me and I'm not going to abandon him.

>CARLY:

You promise?

>DAVID:

I promise.

>*David and Carly move back into the dining room.*

>*In the kitchen a knife gets drawn out of a knife block and begins to move on it's own across the kitchen. As the knife gets past the refrigerator, a murky reflection is seen and it looks like a decaying lady in an old pink ball gown. Once past the fridge, the knife begins to drag along the counter-top.*

INT. - DINING ROOM – NIGHT

>*Amy who is standing closest to the kitchen doesn't notice.*

>*David eventually manages to get Carly to come back with him to Amy. As their walking back the knife continues to move towards Amy's back. They don't notice as the knife drags along the counter. Once the knife gets close enough it raises in the air to strike Amy in the back.*

>*David sees the raised knife and dives for Amy.*

>*He manages to push her out of the way just as the knife comes down.*

>*The knife puts a scratch down Amy's back and both David and Amy tumble to the floor.*

>*Carly begins to scream.*

>*David and Amy manage to stand back up and the knife raises for another strike.*

>*The three of them run off in the hopes of losing the floating knife. They run into the foyer.*

INT. - FOYER - NIGHT

>AMY:

What do we do?

>DAVID:

I don't know.

>AMY:

Can't you fight it off?

>DAVID:

If it's anything like that ghost that grabbed Greg, then I can't.

>AMY:

We have to do something.

INT. - BASEMENT - NIGHT

Greg is bound to the ceiling by his arms in an unknown room.

He takes a look around and sees a table with a stool on the far side of the room and what look like a stone slab altar in the middle. There is dried blood all over the altar but none of it looks new.

He looks around some more and sees some skeletons hanging from the roof in the same manner he is tied up. He tries to break free but the ropes won't move.

He tries to kick his feet but they too are tied down. He gives up with a grunt of frustration.

GREG:
Hello? ...
(silence)
...Is anyone there?...Hello?

Greg watches as the witch comes from behind a corner carrying a pair of pliers. He can hear her mumbling to herself but can't make out what she is saying.

GREG:
Hey, help me.

WITCH:
It must work this time.

GREG:
What?

WITCH:
Or else she will be angry.

GREG:
What must work? Who will be angry?

WITCH:
She needs her tribute.

GREG:
Tribute? What are you talking about tribute?

The witch continues to move closer.

GREG:
C'mon lady, just let me go. I won't tell anyone you're here. Just let me and my friends go and we won't come back. We'll never bother you again and you can continue on whatever it is you're working on and get it right.

WITCH:
I need an ingredient.

GREG:
Ingredient? I can get you any ingredient you want, let me go and I'll go to the store and get it for you.

WITCH:
They do not understand, but they soon will.

The witch bends down to Greg's feet and pulls off one of the socks. Greg looks in horror as the witch puts the pliers on one of his toe-nails.

GREG:
No lady, you don't have to do this, we can work something out.

The Witches House
   Greg screams as the witch pulls the toe-nail out.

   GREG:
No please, just let me go. I'll do anything.

   WITCH:
I'll be back for more ingredient's later.

INT. - FOYER – NIGHT

   The knife comes into the foyer and begins to make it's way across the room. Amy, David and Carly hold each other and start screaming.

   As the knife passes by the mirror in the foyer, it stops. The group look towards the mirror and can now see the woman in the pink dress. The ghost looks at itself and then lets out a scream and vanishes.

   The knife drops where it was and clatters on the ground.

   CARLY:
What the?

   AMY:
Did you see that?

   DAVID:
Yeah, yeah I did.

   AMY:
You think they're afraid of their own reflection?

   DAVID:
It's possible, but I don't know. Hey do you have a small mirror with you?

   AMY:
Yeah of course, it's in my suitcase...
   (pause)
...Do you think it would work?

   DAVID:
It's worth a try.

   Amy starts going through her luggage.

   AMY:
It's a rather small mirror though, I don't know if I'd be able to get the whole reflection in it.

DAVID:
I said it was worth a try didn't I?

   AMY:
Don't take that tone with me.

   DAVID:
Sorry, I'm just frustrated.

   AMY:
Same here, but still.

   DAVID:
We may have a fighting chance now.

CARLY:
A fighting chance to do what?

DAVID:
To find Greg.

CARLY:
Are you serious? Then what are we waiting for?

Amy gets done in her luggage and pulls out a small purse sized mirror.

INSERT – THE MIRROR

BACK TO THE FOYER

AMY:
Here, this is all I got.

Amy gives the mirror to David.

DAVID:
Let's hope it works as well as that one on the wall.

CARLY:
Too bad we couldn't take that one with us.

DAVID:
I'm not Hercules, this small one will have to do.

CARLY:
Let's hope it works.

They begin to walk down the right hand hallway.

The hallway is lined with rugs and doors that stretch down the entire length of the hall. On the walls are paintings of flowers, landscapes and some of tigers and elephants.

The pictures themselves are moving, the flowers growing and dying, the landscapes sun and moon going across the sky, the tigers prowling through the grass and the elephants feeding.

As the group approaches each painting it continues to move as if alive.

CARLY:
Those paintings are freaking me out.

David tries to check behind the paintings.

DAVID:
There's nothing behind them.

AMY:
They're just another one of the features of this place.

CARLY:
Do you think that was why the village we passed through was so dead? Do you think this house sucked the life and people right out of it?

AMY:
I don't think so, I did talk to someone remember.

CARLY:
True.

The Witches House
DAVID:
I'm going to try and see if there's anything in one of these rooms.

AMY:
Alright, but be careful.

DAVID:
Aren't I always?

AMY:
Don't get me started.

DAVID:
True, I am dating you.

AMY:
Hey.

Amy gives David a quick jab to the shoulder.

David opens up the first door and it opens up to a maid's quarters. He looks around and finds a bed, a dresser and an open closet but that is all. The room is empty.

The drapes are closed but David goes to open the drapes. As he does so another ghost, this one in a maids uniform appears from behind the drapes.

DAVID:
Shit.

AMY:
(yelling)
The mirror. Use the mirror.

David tries to bring the mirror up to the ghost but it is knocked away before he is able to bring the mirror up.

AMY:
What did you do?

DAVID:
She knocked it away from me.

AMY:
Well get it back.

David backs off from the ghost but the ghost tries to chase him down. The ghost swings with her arm at him but David is able to get out of the way. David and Amy both back out of the room and the ghost continues to follow them.

Carly stays where she is too scared to do anything but scream.

AMY:
(yelling)
Carly, get the mirror.

Carly screams.

DAVID:
Get the mirror. Hurry up.

CARLY:
I...I can't.

AMY:
You have to.

Carly moves carefully over the mirror and picks it up.

CARLY:
(quietly)
Hey...hey ghost.

DAVID:
You gotta get it's attention!

The ghost grabs David and throws him up against the wall in the hallway. Amy begins to scream not knowing what to do.

Carly is suddenly standing behind the ghost.

CARLY:
(loudly)
I said...hey ghost.

The ghost looks at its' reflection, screams and then fades away.

Amy walks up to David.

AMY:
How about we don't open up anymore random doors.

DAVID:
Sorry, was just looking for Greg.

AMY:
Well let's try and look around first.

DAVID:
Sounds like a plan.

Carly gives the mirror back to David.

CARLY:
Here, I don't want to have to do that again.

AMY:
No worries babe, you did well.

CARLY:
Can we just find Greg and get out of here?

AMY:
Of course.

They walk to the end of the hallway where the find a staircase that leads to a basement floor.

A haunting wind sound can be heard coming up from the basement.

CARLY:
Do you think he's down there?

DAVID:
It's possible.

The Witches House

CARLY:
Should we go check it out?

AMY:
I don't think that's a wise move. There's not a lot of light down there.

CARLY:
But what if he's down there?

DAVID:
Tell you what, if we don't find him anywhere else in the house, we'll go check down there okay?

CARLY:
But what if he's dead by then?

AMY:
I have a feeling that if he was dead he already would be.

CARLY:
(cries)
How can you say that?

AMY:
Sorry I didn't mean it like that.

CARLY:
If I wasn't so scared I'd go down there and search for him myself.

DAVID:
I promise we'll go down there, when and if we need to.

CARLY:
Alright.

They start to head down the hallway towards the foyer when one of the doors bursts open and the witch comes through and drags Carly through the door kicking and screaming.

CARLY:
Help me.

David and Amy manage to grab on to Carly's legs before she is dragged off.

They pull as hard as they can but they start to lose Carly to the strength of the witch.

DAVID:
Damn that thing is strong.

AMY:
Hang on hun, we got you.

CARLY:
(crying)
Please help me.

DAVID:
Just hang on, we'll save you.

With a final pull the witch breaks David and Amy's grasp and Carly is pulled into the room.

David and Amy run into the room trying to find Carly but there is no sign of her.

AMY:
Where'd she go?

DAVID:
I don't know, look for a door or something that thing could have taken her through.

They search the room but find no other doors.

DAVID:
What the hell?

AMY:
(crying)
It's all my fault.

DAVID:
What are you talking about?

AMY:
If I hadn't decided to come up here none of this would be happening.

DAVID:
Don't think like that, you couldn't have known.

David hugs Amy.

AMY:
It's my fault, it's all my fault.

INT. - DARK ROOM – NIGHT

Back to the dark room with the upside down cross. It is again lit with candles and the woman in the black robe is once again on her knees praying. The altar has a woman on it with a knife sticking out of her chest. The blood is flowing all over the altar.

MOM:
Is she worthy my lady?

BLOODY MARY:
She is worthy.

MOM:
I am pleased.

BLOODY MARY:
Now is the appointed time, go to collect the sacrifice.

MOM:
Have the others been prepared?

BLOODY MARY:
Are you questioning me child?

MOM:
No my lady, I am not.

BLOODY MARY:
Then do as your told. I will deal with those you sent by the time you pick up the sacrifice.

MOM:
Yes my lady, whatever pleases you.

The Witches House
Mom gets up and heads out of the room.

INT. - SECOND DARK ROOM – NIGHT

When she gets out of the room she enters into a hallway filled with black robed people. Some of the faces can be seen and they are all women.

PRIESTESS:
What are the lady's wishes?

MOM:
I am to head to the McMann plantation and pick up the sacrifice.

PRIESTESS:
She is pleased then?

MOM:
Yes, the one I chose for her is what she wanted.

The woman takes off her robe and places it down on a table. On the table is a picture frame with a photo of Amy in it. The woman grabs a purse and heads out of the room.

INSERT – PICTURE OF AMY

INT. - HOUSE – BASEMENT – NIGHT

Back to the basement to Carly who is bound by her arms to the ceiling. She looks around and groans. She has some blood flowing from her head. She tries to touch her head and then realizes she is tied up.

CARLY:
Damn it, where am I?

Carly looks around and sees Greg tied up beside her. He is missing a toe-nail from each foot, his right hand and his left ear are also gone. Carly begins to cry.

CARLY:
Greg.

Greg moans.

CARLY:
Greg. What's happened to you?

GREG:
(moaning)
Carly?

CARLY:
Yes, babe, it's me. I'm here. What's going on?

GREG:
You shouldn't be here.

CARLY:
None of us should, but we are.

GREG:
No, you don't understand. She'll kill you.

CARLY:
Who will kill me?

GREG:
Her, the witch.

CARLY:
What witch?

GREG:
The one that took you down here.

CARLY:
I don't understand, what does she want with us?

GREG:
I don't know, she keeps talking about ingredient's and a sacrifice.

CARLY:
You've talked to her?

GREG:
Not really, every time she comes in for her ingredient's, she's mumbling something under her breath.

CARLY:
What does she need ingredient's for?

GREG:
I don't know.

CARLY:
Did she have to take your hand and your ear? Why did she rip you apart like this?

GREG:
She took my ear too? Shit, must have taken it when I passed out.

CARLY:
What did you pass out from?

GREG:
From her taking off my hand.

CARLY:
Didn't you try to fight her?

GREG:
The bitch is strong and fast. When she untied my hand to cut it off, I tried to fight her but she quickly got hold of it and cut if off. After that I blacked out. I didn't come out of it until you started calling my name.

WITCH:
(from a distance)
She's not the one, no she isn't.

CARLY:
What is she talking about?

GREG:
I don't know, something about a chosen sacrifice. Someone is supposed to come that she's been waiting for.

CARLY:
Any idea who this person is?

The Witches House
GREG:
No, I don't

CARLY:
Have you asked her? You said she talks.

GREG:
Yes she does, but not at you, it's more like mindless rambling.

The witch enters the room.

CARLY:
Excuse me?

WITCH:
They like to talk they do, that must change.

CARLY:
What do you want from us?

WITCH:
They do not understand, they will never understand.

CARLY:
What's that supposed to mean?

The witch pulls out a knife and starts to move towards Greg.

GREG:
Oh no, look whatever happens I want you to know something.

CARLY:
Nothing's going to happen, we'll be fine.

GREG:
You don't know that.

CARLY:
Please just hang on Greg, nothing else is going to happen to us. I'm here now.

GREG:
Please just listen to me.

CARLY:
(crying)
I can't, not now we gotta get out of here.

GREG:
I just wanted to say, before she kills me...

CARLY:
You're not going to die.

GREG:
Carly, babe, I love you.

CARLY:
What?

GREG:
I love you.

CARLY:
Now you're saying it?

GREG:
I always have, I was just afraid.

CARLY:
And you're not now?

The witch grabs Greg's head and brings the knife up to his mouth.

GREG:
I've had time to think. I love you Carly, I really do.

The witch forces open Greg's mouth and cuts out his tongue.

CARLY:
(screaming)
No.

WITCH:
All the pieces are almost together. What to do with her I wonder?

CARLY:
You bitch. You beast, how could you?

WITCH:
They do not understand.

The witch leaves the room.

CARLY:
You're a monster, you deserve to die.

Greg begins to cough and spits up blood.

CARLY:
Oh Greg, I'll get you out of here I promise.

Greg just shakes his head.

CARLY:
Yes I will, just you wait.

Carly begins to play with the ropes that are holding her up. She struggles and moans and manages to pull one of her hands free.

CARLY:
Yes, I'm free.

Greg passes out. Carly loosens the rest of the ropes that are holding her.

CARLY:
(to Greg)
I can't carry you babe, but I'll get David and we'll come back for you I promise you.

Carly begins to run for the exit.

She goes into the next room and she sees the next room that is full of bookshelves and scrolls. Other strange things are held in jars that are fastened to the roof. One holds a rat, one a human skull and still another eyeballs.

The Witches House

   Carly attempts to hold back some puke and manages to.

   She quietly tip toes past the witch who has her back turned to her and is sitting at a desk. She can see Greg's hand, tongue and ear on the table. The witch is organizing them and drawing symbols on them.

   When Carly gets into the next room she can hear the witch getting up and heading back into the room where Greg is tied up. Carly starts to move down the hallway she is now in. She can see a set of stairs at the end of the hallway.

CARLY:
I knew, he was down here. Now I just got to find them and we can be out of here.

WITCH (V.O.):
No. Where is she? She must not escape.

CARLY:
Shit.

   Carly begins to run down the hallway towards the set of stairs.

   As she runs she notices there are skeletons lining the hallway that have been picked clean.

   With the witches scream a horde of rats and vermin begin to congregate around Carly and cut off her escape to the stairs.

   Carly picks up a chunk of bone from a nearby skeleton and tries to fight off the rats.

   The sound of the witch pursuing her can be heard.

WITCH:
Get back here. You are mine.

CARLY:
I am no one's. Leave me alone.

WITCH:
You are not the one, you must die.

CARLY:
No.

   The witch swings a knife at Carly but Carly manages to avoid it.

   Carly swings the bone she is holding at the witch and manages to hit her right in the head.

   The witch stumbles back holding on to her head as if in pain.

   The rats clear a path to the stairs as they start to run off

CARLY:
Now leave me and my friends alone.

   Carly starts to head up the stairs.

   As she gets to the top she gets into the hallway but sees no one.

   Suddenly she is pulled from behind and gets stabbed.

   The witch is standing over her smiling.

   The witch pulls the knife and and starts to stab Carly continuously. Blood spews all over the floor.

Carly dies.

The witch then pulls the body back down into the basement.

As she does so the carpet in the upstairs hallway soaks up the blood so that it is gone and no where to be found.

She drags Carly's body back to the room she has Greg in and starts to feast on Carly's flesh.

Greg wakes up in time to see the witch eating Carly. Once she has taken a few mouthfuls of flesh, she waves her hand and rats come in and start to eat away at the corpse. They pick Carly's corpse clean of all flesh and organs then run off.

Greg watches all this then throws up and starts to cry.

WITCH:
She was foolish, yes she was. As all of them are foolish. They will not escape, there is no escape from this house. The lady says so, it is her house and everything in here belongs to her. They need to understand that, even they are hers, they just don't know it yet.

INT. - HALLWAY 2 - NIGHT

Amy and David are now in the hallway on the left side of the foyer.

There are rugs and rooms just like in the right side but there are no paintings. Instead there are portraits. One of them looks just like the store clerk back in the village. One of the pictures have him with some kids and yet another with his wife.

A last portrait is of her by herself. She bears a resemblance to the witch.

Amy is busy looking at the portrait of the store clerk when Carly's scream is heard.

DAVID:
Did you hear that?

AMY:
Carly?

They run into the foyer and then to the other hallway where the paintings are still moving but there is nothing to see, the blood is already soaked into the carpet.

DAVID:
We must have been hearing things.

AMY:
Wouldn't surprise me.

DAVID:
What was so fascinating about that portrait on the wall?

AMY:
It just looks so much like that guy I talked to in the village.

DAVID:
You're really fixated on that aren't you?

AMY:
Well he warned us to stay away from here.

DAVID:
Anyone who has heard rumors about this place would probably warn us to stay away from here.

The Witches House

AMY:

Yeah, but I just find it strange that someone that looks so much like the guy who at one time owned this place would warn us to stay away.

DAVID:

Like I said earlier, it's probably a distant relative.

AMY:

Yeah, but even relatives and children don't look that much alike.

DAVID:

The more you worry about it, the more it'll upset you so just leave it okay?

AMY:

Yeah, alright...
(pause, Amy walks up to David)
...this really sucks huh?

DAVID:

You're just figuring that out now?

AMY:

No I mean, you were supposed to be working right now.

DAVID:

Yeah, it's pretty sad when you'd rather be working.

AMY:

No one except us, knew you were coming though, it was so last minute.

DAVID:

Hey, I would have called in sick to spend time with you. We've barely been able to spend much time together lately and I know that's why you've been a little grumpy lately.

AMY:

Yeah, I'm just sorry I got you into this.

DAVID:

Don't be, it was my choice to come I'm the only one to blame if something happens to us.

AMY:

Do you think they're still alive?

DAVID:

I don't really want to assume anything at this point.

AMY:

C'mon, I really wanna know what you're thinking.

DAVID:

Honestly, no I don't think they're alive...
(Amy starts to cry)
...but we'll look for them all the same just to be sure.

AMY:

I just don't know how much more I can take of this.

DAVID:

I think you're doing well so far.

AMY:

Not as well as you think.

Amy takes the mirror, opens it and starts looking at herself.

AMY:
Damn my make-up is getting all smudged.

DAVID:
You're worrying about your make-up now?

AMY:
Hey can't a girl look good anytime she wants?

DAVID:
You always look good, no matter what.

Amy and David kiss.

AMY:
Thanks, you always know how to make a girl feel special.

DAVID:
It's one of my many gifts.

Amy laughs.

STORE CLERK:
Sorry to bother your special moment here, but may I speak to you?

Amy jumps suddenly and the store clerk sees his reflection in the mirror. He screams then fades away.

DAVID:
Was that they guy you were talking about?

AMY:
Yes, it was.

DAVID:
Oh.

AMY:
Which probably means he is dead or a ghost or whatever these things are.

DAVID:
I don't think he was up to anything good.

AMY:
But he did seem like he wanted to talk to us, and he did forewarn us not to come here.

DAVID:
If it's even the same person, ghost or whatever. It's probably just the spirit of the dead guy in the photo and the guy at the store was his relative.

AMY:
Is it so hard for you to believe they could be the same person?

DAVID:
It just doesn't make any sense to me of how they could be the same person.

AMY:
Does any of this make any sense?

The Witches House
  DAVID:
True, did you want to see if we can find him again?

  AMY:
Sure, if we didn't kill him.

  DAVID:
Let's hope we didn't.

Act 3

INT. - DINING ROOM - NIGHT

Amy and David walk cautiously through the foyer and into the kitchen.

It sounds like mice running along the floor can be heard and it causes Amy to jump. David is startled by the sound but otherwise unaffected.

They continue into the dining room and they look around trying to see any ways out of the room.

DAVID:
Which way do you want to go?

AMY:
I have no idea. He could be anywhere.

DAVID:
I know, I have a feeling this isn't going to be easy.

AMY:
Hopefully he'll be able to help us.

DAVID:
What if he can't? What do you want to do then?

AMY:
I haven't even thought about that.

DAVID:
It's a very real possibility.

AMY:
I realize that, but I'm trying to be positive here.

DAVID:
(shocked)
You?...be positive? Since when?

AMY:
Don't start with that now.

DAVID:
I was only being sarcastic.

AMY:
I don't care, I'm really not in the mood.

DAVID:
Alright, sorry.

AMY:
Let's try up there.

The Witches House

   Amy points to a doorway on the upper right hand side of the dining room.

   David shrugs his shoulders and the two of them start heading for the doorway.

   When they get to the stairs they see a ghost walking through the room.

   Amy gets ready to scream but stops when she realizes it is Carly.

AMY:
Carly? Hun? What happened to you?

   Silence.

AMY:
C'mon talk to me.

   Carly begins to walk and goes right through Amy as though she isn't even there.

AMY:
Oh no, this isn't possible.

DAVID:
I was afraid of this.

AMY:
She's dead, that means Greg probably is too.

DAVID:
Probably.

   Amy cries.

   David walks up and hugs her.

AMY:
So now what?

DAVID:
I guess we just have to find a way out of here.

CARLY:
There is no way out.

AMY:
Excuse me?

CARLY:
You're all going to die.

AMY:
Please don't say that.

CARLY:
You might as well give up, it's all going to end for you.

AMY:
That's not true.

CARLY:
If she gets you, you will pray for death.

   Carly vanishes through a wall.

AMY:
I'm not going to give up.

DAVID:
That's what I want to hear...
(hugs Amy)
...we should get going then.

AMY:
Okay.

The two of them let go of each other and head up the stairs to the door.

INT. - LIVING ROOM – NIGHT

They walk through the door into a large living room. Inside there are ghosts but they pay no attention to Amy or David some of them turn to look at them but then go on with what they were doing. Two GHOSTS are sitting on a couch staring forward. Two are talking at a table, while another is walking around the room.

There is a door at the other end of the room in a corner.

AMY:
I think we took the wrong way. You got that mirror on hand?

DAVID:
Yeah, I do.

AMY:
Do think we should use it?

DAVID:
They don't seem to be too worried about us.

AMY:
There's a door over in the far corner, maybe we should try going through there.

DAVID:
We can try, hopefully these things don't give us a hard time.

The two of them begin to walk.

None of the ghosts try to stop them but as they get closer to the door the ghost walking around the room picks up his pace. As they walk by the ghosts on the couch the ghosts turn to look at them, Amy screams but the ghosts just look away as if nothing happened.

When they get within arms reach of the door the ghost that is walking around moves in front of them.

WALKING GHOST:
I'm sorry I can't allow you to leave.

AMY:
What?

WALKING GHOST:
I told you, you're not allowed to leave.

AMY:
Why?

The Witches House

WALKING GHOST:
We've been waiting too long for you and we're not just going to let you go.

AMY:
What are you talking about?

WALKING GHOST:
I wouldn't worry about it.

AMY:
Well I am worried about it.

WALKING GHOST:
Just go offer yourself to the witch and we can all go home.

AMY:
I will do no such thing.

WALKING GHOST:
Then I'm afraid we'll have to take you there.

DAVID:
I don't think so.

The walking ghost lunges at them and David pulls out the mirror and faces towards him.

The walking ghost screams and disappears.

The two talking at the table get up and quickly start hovering over to the Amy and David.

David shows one of the two ghosts the mirror and it disappears. The other ghost screams out a deathly scream and grabs onto Amy.

Amy struggles but doesn't manage to break free.

David circles around behind Amy and opens up the mirror again.

The ghost vanishes.

The two ghosts sitting on the couch get up and start moving towards them.

DAVID:
We need to get out of here.

AMY:
Don't have to tell me twice.

INT. - OFFICE – NIGHT

Amy and David try to open the door and it opens up to a small office. The office is full of the decaying and rotting ghosts.

SITTING GHOST:
You can't kill us.

AMY:
We can try.

SITTING GHOST:
Even with that trinket of yours, you can't kill us.

AMY:
Just let us go.

SITTING GHOST:
I'm sorry, we can't allow that.

David and Amy run for the door back to the dining room.

The ghosts try to stop them but David and Amy are too fast. They manage to run past the ghosts without any harm.

INT. - DINING ROOM – NIGHT

They start to descend down the stairs when David is grabbed from behind.

He drops the mirror and grabs on to the hand railing trying to break himself free.

DAVID:
Get the mirror.

AMY:
Where is it?

DAVID:
On the steps behind you.

Amy fumbles around on the steps but manages to grab the mirror.

She shows it to the ghosts trying to drag David back.

They scream and both disappear.

David falls down and rolls down a few steps before stopping himself.

DAVID:
That was close.

AMY:
Yeah, but we should get moving, there's more coming.

David looks up the stairs and sees more ghosts coming out of the living room.

The two of them get up and run down the stairs and into the kitchen.

INT. - KITCHEN - NIGHT

Different kitchen utensils lift up from their places in the kitchen and start to fly at Amy and David.

They try to duck and dodge as many of them as possible.

Amy manages to get to the other side of the kitchen just fine but David is hit with a knife in his arm. The knife goes in deep and it manages to get some blood to spray out onto the kitchen cupboards as David pulls it out.

INT – FOYER – NIGHT

They run into the foyer.

AMY:
Are you okay?

The Witches House
DAVID:
I think so, it really hurts.

AMY:
You're really bleeding.

DAVID:
We need to get it to stop before I lose too much blood.

Amy looks around quickly.

AMY:
There's nothing around to tie to wound up with.

DAVID:
Here take my shirt and make a bandage with it.

David takes of his shirt to an undershirt.

Amy takes the shirt and ties it over the wound. The blood starts to come through the shirt but the bleeding does stop.

AMY:
How is that?

DAVID:
I guess it'll work...
          (groans in pain)
...I'll probably need stitches if we manage to get out of here.

AMY:
          (frantic)
We'll get out of here, we have to.

DAVID:
I'm starting to have my doubts.

AMY:
Don't say that, I can't hear you say that.

DAVID:
Alright, alright.

The door to the right side of the foyer suddenly bursts open and the witch comes out with her arms out wide.

She grabs David by the shoulders and starts to drag him off.

AMY:
          (screaming)
David.

DAVID:
I got her.

David manages to swing his head backwards and hits the witch in the face.

The witch lets him go and grabs her face screaming.

WITCH:
No, you are not supposed to be here.

DAVID:
How do we get out of here?

WITCH:
You may never leave.

DAVID:
Tell us how to get out.

The witch lunges at David again and grabs at his arm. He manages to pull it away but the witch is too quick and grabs onto his other arm.

David tries to pull it away but the witch is too strong.

He punches his other fist at her head but screams in pain from the knife wound.

WITCH:
You will come with me now.

DAVID:
I don't think so.

David shows her the mirror.

WITCH:
Silly boy, I am no ghost.

Amy comes up behind her with a vase and smashes it over her head.

The witch lets David go and screams.

She disappears into the door again and the door slams shut.

Amy goes to open the door again, when it opens the witch is gone.

WITCH (V.O.):
I'll will find you, and you will be mine, all mine.

Amy goes over to David.

AMY:
Are you okay?

DAVID:
Yeah, that bitch is strong.

AMY:
At least she didn't get you.

DAVID:
Thank you.

AMY:
She looked really familiar.

DAVID:
Yeah, she looked like one of the paintings in that hallway.

David points to the left side hallway.

> *Amy goes and opens the door and starts to head down the hallway to the paintings.*

> *She looks below the one of the witch and there is a name plate there.*

AMY:
Helen Blackhorn.

DAVID:
(standing by the store clerks painting)
And Norman Blackhorn.

AMY:
Those two were husband and wife?

DAVID:
Looks like this is more confusing than we thought.

AMY:
I have an idea...

DAVID:
What's that?

AMY:
(yelling)
Norman...Norman where are you?

DAVID:
What are you doing?

AMY:
Trying to get his attention.

DAVID:
Other things may here you!

AMY:
(yelling)
Norman, we need to talk to you.

> *The store clerk shows up behind Amy.*

STORE CLERK:
I am here.

AMY:
(screams)
What is going on here?

STORE CLERK:
I'm not sure I understand what you mean.

AMY:
With everything,, the ghosts, that woman, this house...how do we get out of here?

STORE CLERK:
Unfortunately there is no real way out.

AMY:
What do you mean?

STORE CLERK:
The only way out is either for you to surrender to the witch or else to kill her.

AMY:
How do we kill her?

STORE CLERK:
As you would any other human being.

AMY:
She's seems to be something more than human.

STORE CLERK:
Yes, the dark pact she made with her gods made her unable to die a natural death. But a knife to the chest would do the trick just fine.

DAVID:
Why would you help us kill your wife?

STORE CLERK:
She was my wife, a long time ago. That is past now and I wish to be free as you are and if she dies then this will all be over, for all of us.

AMY:
How did the other ghosts get here?

STORE CLERK:
They came here the same as you, either on a vacation or else bought the house. The last to purchase the property were the McMann's, hence its' name.

AMY:
So you originally owned this place.

STORE CLERK:
A long time ago yes.

AMY:
What happened, how did you and the others starts haunting this place?

STORE CLERK:
When I married Helen I had no idea that she was a practicing witch. We lived many years happily married, or so I thought. Then one night she came into our bedroom and stabbed me several times in the heart. After I became what I am now I realized that she had started a ritual that lasts until this day. All who die in this house inevitably end up haunting it.

DAVID:
What ritual?

STORE CLERK:
A ritual to unleash an evil spirit.

DAVID:
Is our friend still alive?

STORE CLERK:
The boy? Unfortunately no, he is dead and here with us.

AMY:
So we're the only two left.

STORE CLERK:
Unfortunately, yes.

DAVID:

The ghosts off the dining room mentioned that I wasn't supposed to be here, what did they mean by that?

STORE CLERK:

Everyone that ends up here, the witch knows about before hand. Other witches that are associated with her forewarn her that people are coming and she prepares for them.

DAVID:

What does that have to do with me?

STORE CLERK:

We never knew you were coming. Helen didn't prepare for you, if anything you are a kink in the plan. As a result, Helen will be more determined to kill you, for you are a danger to her.

DAVID:

In what way?

STORE CLERK:

It's a matter of fate and circumstance. They were fated to be here and you were not. You are an agent of chance and not of fate, as a result you could be the key in setting us all free.

AMY:

I don't understand.

STORE CLERK:

Don't worry about it, just realize that you David are feared here. Even the ghosts don't like your presence here.

AMY:

Who are these witches associated with Helen?

STORE CLERK:

Witches that worship Bloody Mary.

AMY:

Isn't she a myth?

STORE CLERK:

Sorry to disappoint you, but she's very real.

DAVID:

Can't they just look in a mirror and say her name three times?

STORE CLERK:

Unfortunately it's more complicated than that.

DAVID:

How so?

STORE CLERK:

They need a worthy sacrifice.

AMY:

You mean me.

STORE CLERK:

Yes.

AMY:

Is this place what happened to the village? Is that why it's so...dead there?

STORE CLERK:
Yes, everyone that lived there at one time was drawn to this house and died here. Many people have tried to repopulate the town but it's always the inevitable end.

DAVID:
Do you think your mom had something to do with this?

AMY:
How dare you even suggest that?

DAVID:
You said she was the one who let us use this house?

AMY:
Why would my own mother send us into a death trap?

DAVID:
How about that friend who you said owns this house? Did she maybe con your mom into letting us use it?

AMY:
That's possible. So what, to get out of here we have to kill the witch?

STORE CLERK:
Yes, and I pray that you do it soon. We've been waiting a long time to move on.

AMY:
We'll do our best.

STORE CLERK:
Thank you.

DAVID:
We better get busy.

Amy and David walk off and the store clerk disappears.

INT. - CAR – NIGHT

The camera fades in to the view of the woman in the black robes. She is now driving down the highway. There is no congestion and the moon is high in the sky.

She is talking on her cellphone.

MOM:
Oh I'm sure she's fine.

Mumbling coming from cellphone.

MOM:
She probably just forgot to call you when she got there. She's on vacation after all. Let her live a little bit.

Mumbling coming from cellphone.

MOM:
Why do you have to try and control her life? You know she'll be moving out of there someday.

Mumbling coming from cellphone.

The Witches House
    MOM:
Well you're going to have to loosen the strings at some point, it doesn't matter if your her father she has to be allowed to live her own life.

    Mumbling coming from cellphone. Mom hangs up cellphone.

    MOM:
I knew there was a good reason why I left him.

INSERT – PICTURE OF AMY ON DASHBOARD

    MOM (V.O.):
Soon, child, soon.

INT. - LEFT HALLWAY - NIGHT

    Amy and David are walking down the hallway where they found the portraits and talked to the store clerk.

    AMY:
Do you have anything on you we can use as a weapon?

    DAVID:
No, I don't. There's those knives in the kitchen, one of them has to be good enough to stab her with.

    AMY:
Sure, let's go check it out.

    Just as they are about to walk past the last door, the door bursts open and witch grabs David in a choke hold.

    He fights back but is unable to break free.

    AMY:
    (yelling)
David.

    DAVID:
Hit her.

    AMY:
With what?

    DAVID:
I don't know just hit her.

    Amy goes up and punches the witch right in the head. The witch isn't affected at all.

    WITCH:
Foolish child thinks they can get away from me.

    AMY:
Let him go.

    DAVID:
Just go get the knives. I'll fight her off best I can.

    AMY:
No, I won't leave you.

    The witch starts to manage to drag David off into the room.

David drops the mirror.

INSERT – THE MIRROR

BACK TO LEFT HALLWAY

DAVID:
You have to.

AMY:
I can't.

DAVID:
Go, I'll be alright.

AMY:
No.

The witch pulls David into the room and then everything falls silent.

Amy goes into the room to see where they went and there is no sign of them. The room is a small bedroom with an antique single bed and a wardrobe in a corner.

Amy searches throughout the entire room and finds no evidence of trapdoors or hidden passageways.

AMY:
(starts to cry)
David, I love you, I hope you know that.

Silence.

AMY:
Okay, knives, if he's still alive, I have to help him.

Amy leaves the room.

INT. - KITCHEN – NIGHT

Amy runs into the kitchen frantically and starts fumbling around with the knives she tests the edges of the knives and gets the sharpest ones she can find.

She turn around to go back into the foyer and a ghost is standing right beside her.

Amy screams.

The ghost swings at her but Amy manages to avoid the hit.

She backs off towards the dining room not seeing the ghosts coming through the door.

She turns around and sees five ghosts coming from behind her.

She runs along the other side of the kitchen. All the utensils that went flying at her before come back to life and she runs as fast as she can.

AMY:
The mirror...
(feels around for the mirror)
...where's the mirror? Shit. I hope it's not still on David.

Amy goes to run but is tripped up by a ghost. She realizes she is being held down and is starting to be dragged back.

The Witches House
> *She tries to stab the ghosts but the blade passes right through all of them.*

> *With one final feat of strength, Amy pulls and manages to free herself.*

> *She gets up and runs as fast as she can towards the foyer.*

> *A ghost just barely misses her as she runs by.*

> *Amy runs into the foyer and the ghosts are on her tail. She run across the room to the hallway. The ghosts go past the giant mirror without looking at it.*

> *Amy goes into the hallway and sees the mirror laying on the floor. She picks it up, opens it and shows it to a ghost that is right behind her.*

> *The ghost screams and vanishes.*

> *The rest of the ghosts realize she has a mirror and vanish soon after the other ghost.*

AMY:
Keep that on me just in case...
> *(puts mirror in pocket)*
...Okay, David I'm coming for you, just hang in there.

> *Amy walks over to the stairs and starts to head down.*

INT. - BASEMENT – NIGHT

> *David is laying on the floor. His hands and feet are tied so he is unable to sit up when he tries.*

> *He looks around and sees Greg's corpse hanging from the ceiling.*

> *He rolls over and throws up.*

> *When he's done he looks and sees the dressed skeleton of Amy. At first he doesn't recognize the body but after looking at the clothes he recognizes it with a look of shock.*

DAVID:
Amy, what did she do to you? And Greg, I can't even think about that without feeling sick.

> *Rummaging around is heard in the next room.*

DAVID:
Hello? Helen? Is that you?

WITCH (V.O.):
He tries to talk to me he does.

DAVID:
C'mon Helen, let's talk this out.

> *David tries to fumble with the ropes but they won't loosen for him.*

DAVID:
You don't have to do this Helen.

WITCH (V.O.):
He knows nothing, he is young and foolish.

DAVID:
We won't tell anyone if you let us go, you can continue to live forever, I promise you.

WITCH:
His promises are empty, yes. Remember what happened last time you let someone go.

DAVID:
What? What happened last time?

WITCH:
He still asks questions, we should silence him.

DAVID:
No, please don't I won't say anymore.

The witch comes into the room and moves towards him.

She kneels down and begins to strangle him.

WITCH:
You are not supposed to be here. You are sickness to me, disease, and I will cure you from me.

DAVID:
(chocking)
It was last minute, I swear, we didn't know.

WITCH:
No one knows, no one is supposed to know.

She stops chocking David.

WITCH:
But we still have uses for you, yes, you will do nicely.

DAVID:
(coughs)
What uses?

The witch walks away.

DAVID:
Hey. What uses?

INT. - BASEMENT HALLWAY - NIGHT

Amy gets to the bottom of the stairs and looks around. She is shocked by the skeletons that are laying around and covers her mouth as though she is about to throw up. She swallows it down and starts to move down the hallway.

She is being cautious, looking around, holding the knives up, trying to be prepared for anything that may jump out of the shadows at her.

She screams when she is suddenly stopped by the ghost of Carly, who now looks rotting and decayed.

AMY:
Carly honey, I'm so sorry.

Carly snarls then starts to walk towards Amy.

AMY:
No Carly, you're better than this, you have to help me.

Carly jabs at Amy but Amy jumps out of the way.

The Witches House

AMY:

Remember that time as kids that we promised to be friends forever? That promise is still good. I can help you be free, any friend would help out a friend right?

Carly, grabs on to Amy and throws her to the ground.

AMY:

Please honey, I'm your friend, and I'm here for you now.

A look of recognition crosses Carly's face.

She tries to shake it off and snarls some more but then she stops.

Carly screams looking like she's fighting some internal torment.

Carly's ghost runs off towards the stairs runs up them and disappears.

AMY:

Thank you Carly, I just hope I can uphold my promise.

INT. - BASEMENT - NIGHT

The witch enters the room and kneels down to David, she is holding the pair of pliers she used on Greg.

DAVID:

No, what are you doing? No, don't do it.

WITCH:

We must, need ingredients.

DAVID:

What ingredients?

WITCH:

He asks questions again. He should not be so curious.

DAVID:

C'mon, I can get you what you want. Just don't hurt me.

WITCH:

He is foolish if he thinks he can outsmart me.

DAVID:

You're right, I can't outsmart you. You're much smarter than me, please let me help you.

WITCH:

Wise, yet foolish.

The witch leans over grabs his hand and yanks out a fingernail. Blood wells up over the wound and David screams out.

Amy suddenly appears in the doorway.

AMY:

Hey. Leave him alone.

WITCH:

You should not be here, do not interfere.

Amy runs up and tries to stab the witch, but the witch is too fast and runs behind Greg's body.

Amy sees the mangled hanging corpse and begins to gag.

WITCH:
Yes, she is weak. She can not beat me.

Amy goes to cut David free.

DAVID:
No don't worry about me, just get her.

AMY:
But I need your help.

The witch lunges and hit Amy right in the head.

Amy tumbles back on top of Carly's remains. Amy looks around and shrieks once she sees she fallen on her friends remains.

WITCH:
Fool.

David leans up onto his shoulder then spins and uses both legs to kick the witch in her knees.

The witch falls with a crack, shrieking and vanishes into the shadows.

Amy seeing her opportunity gets up and picks up the knives.

She goes over to David and cuts him free.

AMY:
Are you okay?

DAVID:
Where'd she go?

AMY:
I don't know, but we need to get out of here.

DAVID:
I don't think she is just going to let us leave.

The witch lunges out of the darkness and punches Amy in the face causing her to stumble back.

David hits the witch in the stomach but the witch doesn't seem hurt by it.

The witch instead starts to strangle David.

Amy sees what is going on and tries to stab the witch, the witch dodges the attack and David falls back to the ground.

David begins coughing.

AMY:
(yelling)
I could really use your help right now.

DAVID:
I can't breathe.

AMY:
Try.

The Witches House
> *David gets up and tries to grab the witch.*

> *She punches David and he stumbles back.*

> *He grabs a knife out of Amy's hand and readies it to strike her with.*

> *The witch throws Amy against the far wall and Amy falls to the ground unconscious.*

> *David sees this and anger crosses his face.*

> *The witch starts to laugh.*

DAVID:
It's not funny.

> *David stabs the witch.*

> *The witch shrieks then runs off into the shadows. David tries to chase her but he run straight into a wall.*

> *David goes to check on Amy.*

DAVID:
C'mon girl, wake up.

> *Amy doesn't respond.*

DAVID:
C'mon, wake up. I can't lose you not now, not like this. I love you too much for that to happen.

AMY:
(wakes up)
I love you too.

DAVID:
We got to get out of here. We'll have an easier time upstairs in the open.

AMY:
She's not dead yet?

DAVID:
No, I wounded her, but that was it. She ran off into a sold wall.

AMY:
That's crazy.

DAVID:
I know, but it's true. Are you okay to walk.

> *Amy gets up. She stumbles once she's up and David catches her.*

DAVID:
Whoa, easy there tiger.

AMY:
Please don't call me that.

DAVID:
(laughs)
Okay, but we should get moving.

Amy and David begin to move through the basement. As they get towards the stairs rats begin to fill in behind them. The rats don't attack they just watch and move as the two of them go up the stairs. Once they are up the stairs the rats disperse.

INT. - FOYER - DAY

Amy and David stumble through the hallway towards the foyer. Once they get into the foyer, Amy tries to open the front door, it is still locked.

AMY:
Well, I was hoping.

The witch is suddenly at the top of the stairs holding a long curved knife with dried blood on it.

WITCH:
No. They can not leave, they must stay here.

Amy and David both take a knife and prepare for a fight.

DAVID:
Are you okay to fight?

AMY:
No, but we don't have much a choice do we?

DAVID:
True.

The witch jumps off the balcony and lands in the middle of the foyer.

Ghosts start to fill in from the doors. They don't interfere however, they just stand by and watch.

WITCH:
They will see now, they will all see that they must stay here forever.

The witch charges at Amy and David and swings her knife. She manages to slice a cut across Amy's arm.

Amy cries in pain and stumbles back.

David goes to stab the witch but misses.

The witch smiles and backhands David, he falls back into Amy.

WITCH:
They can not defeat me, they got lucky they did, but not again.

DAVID:
Yes, we will.

The witch lunges at them again this time catching David in the shoulder.

David drops to one knee and then the witch slashes him across the face.

Amy screams and David falls to the floor with a large gash across his face.

AMY:
(crying)
No.

Amy moves up to guard David and the witch approaches with her blade high above her head.

The Witches House

 The witch starts to bring her blade down, but Amy reacts quicker and puts the blade through the witches throat.

 The witch gurgles out some blood then falls to the floor dead.

 The ghosts vanish.

 AMY:
We did it, David, we did it, she's gone.

 DAVID:
I'm sorry.

 AMY:
For what?

 DAVID:
Getting myself hurt.

 AMY:
You'll be fine.

 DAVID:
No I won't.

 AMY:
Don't be foolish, it's just a small cut.

 DAVID:
I'm feeling cold and can't move.

 AMY:
We'll fix you, I promise.

 DAVID:
No, you can't, please don't lie to me.

 AMY:
I can't lose you.

 DAVID:
It's too late for that.

 AMY:
Don't say that.

 DAVID:
It's the truth. I'm just happy I could spend my last moments with you.

 AMY:
At least you won't be stuck here forever.

 DAVID:
I have you to thank for that.

 AMY:
You're welcome.

 DAVID:
I was going to ask you something this weekend too.

AMY:
And what was that?

DAVID:
I was going to ask you to marry me.

AMY:
I would have said yes.

DAVID:
Would you still?

AMY:
Yes.

The front door handle turns and the door creaks open. Light from the morning sun floods the foyer.

DAVID:
Go and remember I'll always love you.

David falls unconscious.

Amy tries to find a pulse but fails. She cries.

Wiping away tears, she walks to the front door and lets the sun flood her face.

EXT. - HOUSE – DAY

Amy steps outside and sees Mom standing on the front porch.

AMY:
Mom? What are you doing here?

MOM:
Your father called said he was worried since you never called him. He didn't know how to get here so I came out to make sure you were alright.

AMY:
Mom, thank God you're here.

MOM:
What happened?

AMY:
They're dead, they're all dead.

MOM:
Who is?

AMY:
David, Carly and Greg. My closest friends are dead.

MOM:
I'm sorry honey.

Mom hugs Amy.

AMY:
I should call the police.

The Witches House

MOM:
Don't worry about that. Let's just go home and deal with this when we get there. That sound good?

AMY:
Yeah alright.

MOM:
You're safe now. You have nothing to worry about.

AMY:
Mom?

MOM:
Hmm?

AMY:
You didn't know anything about this place did you?

MOM:
Like what?

AMY:
About ghosts and witches?

MOM:
Oh don't be ridiculous, of course I didn't. If I had even known that kind of stuff was here I wouldn't have sent you.

AMY:
So you don't think I'm crazy?

Mom hugs Amy.

MOM:
Of course not, honey, of course not.

Mom smiles evilly.

Act 4

EXT. - CAR – DAY

    Amy is sitting in her Mom's car. They are pulling away from the house.

    As they pull away from the house the image of the beautiful house fades and it shows itself to be a ruin with the windows gone, the roof partially caved in and the walls mostly overgrown with vines.

INT. - CAR – DAY

    Amy looks depressed and defeated.

    AMY:
What about my car?

    MOM:
We'll come back and get it.

    AMY:
I feel bad leaving the bodies of my friends behind.

    MOM:
We'll call the police when we get home and they'll come around and pick them up.

    AMY:
Okay.
    (silence)
What are you going to say to your friend?

    MOM:
About what?

    AMY:
    (angrily)
About this place, this death trap she sent us to?

    MOM:
I'll speak to her, I'm pretty sure she didn't know anything about this either.

    AMY:
Well somebody knew, and that somebody should be turned into the police.

    MOM:
Don't be so rash, nobody is responsible.

    AMY:
    (angrily)
How can you say that? There had to be somebody that knew about this place.

    MOM:
I'm sure it's not that simple.

The Witches House

AMY:
How can you defend them? Does what happened mean nothing to you?

MOM:
Don't say that.

AMY:
Well it's obviously true.

MOM:
Get some rest dear, you've had a long night.

AMY:
Fine, but this isn't over.

MOM:
(smiles evilly)
No, no it isn't.

INT. - FOYER – DAY

Back to the now ruined foyer of the house. The sun is shining through the ceiling and birds can be heard chirping through the rafters. A gentle breeze blows through the house and a moan is heard.

David reaches up and touches his head, he gasps and sits up. Looking around he is shocked to find he is still alive.

DAVID:
Amy?
(silence)
Amy are you here?

The sounds of a car pulling away are heard. David runs to the closest window and sees Amy's mom's car pulling away.

DAVID:
(yelling)
Amy. Don't leave.

The car pulls away.

DAVID:
Shit.

Sits down on the floor.

DAVID:
That was her mom's car .. what is her mom doing here? Oh no, how'd she know that...I got to help Amy. Looks out the window.

DAVID:
Amy's car is still here.

Holds his face in pain.

DAVID:
Suck it up David.

Gets up looks out the window again and sees Amy's car.

DAVID:
Why didn't she take her car instead? Oh well, at least I have a ride.

David goes outside and into the car.

He searches around for a key and finds one in the visor over the drivers side. He puts it in the ignition and starts the car.

Looking around again he finds a cellphone sitting in the cup holder. David drives off.

EXT. - DAVID'S HOUSE - DAY

David pulls up to his house. He gets out of the car.

DAVID:
Home sweet home.

David gets his key out of his pocket and approaches the front door. He puts his key in the lock and unlocks the door. He then quietly goes inside.

INT. - DAVID'S HOUSE – DAY

Once inside the house is a mess. There are clothes on the floor and fast food wrappers on the couch and coffee table. His DAD, is sitting in a chair in front of the TV completely passed out. A bottle of vodka is in his hands.

David shakes his head and heads into a bedroom that leads off the living room.

DAVID:
Where does he keep it. I know it's here somewhere.

David looks around the room and can't find what he's looking for.

He opens the closet door and winces when a loud creak is heard, Dad stirs but falls back asleep.

David searches around the closet for a few seconds.

DAVID:
There it is.

David pulls out a handgun with a box of ammunition.

He loads up the gun with ammo then puts the box back in the closet.

He puts the gun in his pants and hangs his shirt over the gun so no one will see it.

DAD:
That you boy?

David startles.

DAVID:
Yeah dad it's me.

DAD:
I thought you were supposed to be gone for the weekend.

DAVID:
We came back early.

DAD:
What're you doing in my bedroom boy?

The Witches House

DAVID:
I was just looking for something.

DAD:
Looking for what? I hope you don't have my gun boy.

DAVID:
No, I'm not looking for your gun. I was looking for a change of clothes for you. You look like you haven't changed in days.

DAD:
That's true, I haven't. But I'm okay boy, don't worry about me.

DAVID:
Alright, if you say so.

DAD:
Did you have a good trip boy?

DAVID:
Nah, it wasn't that great.

DAD:
Why's that?

DAVID:
I don't want to talk about it.

DAD:
Why?

DAVID:
(agitated)
I just don't, now if you don't mind I got places I need to be.

David starts to walk out.

DAD:
Hey. Don't you walk out on me boy.

Dad passes out.

David runs out to the car and gets in. A tear rolls down his face.

INT. - CAR – DAY

DAVID:
Dad why do you do this to yourself?

David wipes away the tear then picks up the cellphone.

He scrolls through the contact list and finds one labeled "Dad."

He pushes the call button. The phone rings a few times before TOM answers.

TOM:
Hello?

DAVID:
Hey Tom, it's David.

TOM:
David? Amy's boyfriend?

DAVID:
That's right.

TOM:
What're you doing calling me? Is everything alright?

DAVID:
Not really.

TOM:
Do you need me to come down to the house?

DAVID:
No, I'm back from the house.

TOM:
Where are you?

DAVID:
In town.

TOM:
Where's Amy?

DAVID:
I don't know and I'm hoping you may be able to help.

TOM:
Is she in trouble?

DAVID:
Yeah, I think she is.

TOM:
What kind of trouble?

DAVID:
I'm not sure. The house was a trap for us and I think her mom had something to do with it.

TOM:
A trap? What kind of trap?

DAVID:
Well, two of my close friends are dead and I'm afraid Amy may be soon too if I don't get to her.

TOM:
That bitch. What was she up to now?

DAVID:
I don't know, but I'm hoping to stop her.

TOM:
How can I help?

DAVID:
When you two were married did her mom ever practice any kind of witchcraft?

TOM:
What? That's crazy. I've never heard of her practicing such stuff.

DAVID:
Okay, sorry, was there a place she spent a lot of time at? Like a friends or a hall or something?

TOM:
Yeah, she was always going over to CHAROLETTE'S. I tried asking her what she was doing there, but she never told me. Maybe she was practicing her witchcraft there, if what you're hinting at is true.

DAVID:
Okay, how do I get there?

David starts writing it down.

TOM:
Go down Main Street, to 3rd. Hang a left, go down five blocks to Charles Crescent, take a right and it's the second house on the left.

DAVID:
Okay, thanks.

TOM:
Hey kid...

DAVID:
Yeah?

TOM:
You rescue my little girl.

DAVID:
I'm going to try my hardest.

EXT. - CHAROLETTE'S HOUSE – DAY

Amy and her mom pull up to a house on a quiet street. It is a large house with a garden in the front yard. Children are in the street laughing and playing.

Amy wakes up and looks around.

AMY:
Where are we?

MOM:
Charolette's

AMY:
Why are we here?

MOM:
This is the friend who lent you the house.

AMY:
Oh mom, I really don't feel like talking to her.

MOM:
Oh I insist. Let's deal with this now.

AMY:
Can we do it another day when I've had more sleep? I can barely think straight right now.

MOM:
No, I'd rather do it now.

AMY:
Oh for crying out loud. Fine let's go.

Amy and her mom get out of the car.

They cross the street having to move around the children. They walk up the front steps and ring the doorbell.

A woman answers the door.

MOM:
Hi, Charolette, may we come in?

CHAROLETTE:
(smiles)
Why of course.

Charolette opens the door and a group of four women are in the house. Once Amy comes fully into the house she is grabbed from behind.

INT. - CHAROLETTE'S HOUSE – DAY

AMY:
What's going on?

The women tie her hands and her feet.

MOM:
Take her down to the basement.

CHAROLETTE:
Yes, mistress.

AMY:
What the hell is going on?

The women don't say anything. They carry Amy down the dark room that has the altar and the candles.

INT. - DARK ROOM – DAY

They place her on the altar and tie her down so she can't move. Mom comes down the stairs and stops before entering the room.

Mom strips down naked and puts on the black robe with the gold decorations.

AMY:
Mom what's going on?

MOM:
I haven't been totally honest with you, dear.

AMY:
Ya think?

MOM:
I knew about the house. In fact I own the house.

AMY:
What? Why did you send us there?

The Witches House
MOM:
I needed to prove that you were worthy.

AMY:
Worthy? Worthy of what? Being a sacrifice to Bloody Mary?

MOM:
Precisely.

AMY:
I don't understand why you're doing this.

MOM:
You are to be her chalice which she will drink to her hearts content.

AMY:
You couldn't have chosen someone else for this?

MOM:
No dear, it had to be you.

Mom picks up a curved dagger from a nearby table. The six women and Charolette enter in through the door and close it.

AMY:
I still don't understand why you're doing this.

MOM:
We are bringing order to this chaotic world. Order that will set things right.

AMY:
I don't want anything to do with this, please let me go.

MOM:
I'm sorry, I love you, but I love her more.

Mom points to a statue that is revealed as the women light the candles. It is a woman dressed in robes carrying a child by its' foot in one hand and a dagger in the other. The statue has a sinister look on her face.

AMY:
You can't be serious.

MOM:
Oh, I'm very serious.

AMY:
And when I'm dead? Then what?

MOM:
Then the goddess will enter into this world and bless us all.

AMY:
You're insane.

MOM:
That's what your father said when I left him.

AMY:
He was right.

MOM:
Quiet now dear.

Mom gags Amy.

MOM:
We are ready to begin.
(in Latin)
Come to us dark lady.

WOMEN:
(in Latin)
Yes come.

MOM:
(in Latin)
Come and bless us your servants.

WOMEN:
(in Latin)
Yes come.

The door to the room opens and David is standing there with a gun raised.

DAVID:
Let her go.

Amy looks and screams.

MOM:
Who is this?

DAVID:
Your daughters fiance.

MOM:
You should not be here.

DAVID:
I said let her go, I won't ask again.

Mom points at David.

MOM:
Kill him.

Two of the women draw daggers out of the sleeves of their robes and move towards David.

David shoots one of the women and she falls to the ground. The other three start circling around him.

Mom thrusts her hands out towards David.

He goes to shoot another woman but the gun just clicks.

MOM:
Looking for these?

Mom opens her hand to reveal the bullets to the gun.

DAVID:
How in the...?

The Witches House
    MOM:
You're in over your head here boy.

    The women lunge at David but he dodges their attacks.

    He rolls on the ground and scoops up the dagger from the woman he shot.

    He stands back up and brings the dagger up ready to attack.
Another woman lunges at David, he steps to the side and drives his dagger into her chest.

    The woman falls and dies.

    Mom turns back to Amy.

    MOM:
    (in Latin)
Come to us I pray.

    DAVID:
Stop. Let her go.

    MOM:
Rise dark queen, rise.

    Mom stabs Amy.

    DAVID:
    (cries)
No.

    The women begin to laugh. The two lunge at him but he doesn't give a fight. They don't stab him but hold him to the ground.

    David just watches as Amy's mom drinks some of Amy's blood.

    MOM:
Now is the time. We have done as we have been asked.

    BLOODY MARY (V.O.):
Yes you have done well good and faithful servant.

    MOM:
Come to us and restore your order.

    BLOODY MARY (V.O.):
Prepare for me and I will come.

    Mom turns and looks into a mirror.

    MOM:
Bloody Mary.

    A sinister laughing can be heard. David looks at Amy, Amy's eye look back at him. He can see that she is still alive.

    MOM:
Bloody Mary.

    He squeezes his fists together and fights to get loose. The women are so in awe that they barely notice him throwing them to the ground.

MOM:
Bloody...

DAVID (V.O.):
Die you bitch.

INSERT – MOM'S NECK

A knife point comes out of the front of Mom's neck. Blood shoots out with it.

BACK TO DARK ROOM

Mom collapses.

The women all gasp for a second and then start to circle David. He holds up the knife and they all back off and run out of the room. The room starts to shake and David takes Amy off the altar and carries her through the collapsing house to the front garden.

INT. - HOSPITAL – DAY

Amy is in bed and David is by her side.

Amy wakes up.

AMY:
Ugh, how long have I been out for?

DAVID:
A couple of days.

AMY:
What happened?

DAVID:
You're mom stabbed you.

AMY:
She what? Where is she?

DAVID:
Sorry, Amy, she's dead.

AMY:
(shocked)
How?

DAVID:
After she stabbed you, I stabbed her.

AMY:
How did I survive?

DAVID:
The doctors said that your mom missed any of your major organs. Although it was bleeding quite a bit, if treated it wasn't fatal.

AMY:
You think that was intentional?

DAVID:
Maybe, but I didn't know that at the time.

The Witches House

AMY:
I'm not blaming you for killing her. I would have done the same in your shoes.

DAVID:
I know.

AMY:
What about the other women?

DAVID:
The police said that Charolette and the other women are being charged with Carly and Greg's deaths along with attempted murder for what they did to you.

AMY:
They'll probably never see the light of day again.

DAVID:
Probably not.

AMY:
I'm so sorry I got you into all this.

DAVID:
There's no need to apologize. If I wasn't there, you'd be dead. So I think it was a good thing I was there with you.

AMY:
I still have a hard time understanding how my mom could do this to me.

DAVID:
I don't understand it either, maybe we never will.

AMY:
(sarcastically)
That's oh so comforting.

DAVID:
Well I should let you get some rest.

AMY:
Hey, excuse me?

DAVID:
Yeah?

AMY:
Don't I get a kiss from my fiance?

David smiles, then pulls a ring box from his pocket. He opens it up to reveal a diamond ring.

Amy begins to cry.

He slips the ring on her finger.

DAVID:
Of course you do.

AMY:
I love you.

DAVID:
I love you too.

INT. - HOSPITAL ROOM 2 -- DAY

Mom is laying in a hospital bed, she suddenly wakes up and smiles.

END